LITTLE TIGER PRESS
An imprint of Magi Publications
1 The Coda Centre, 189 Munster Road,
London SW6 6AW
First published in Great Britain 2000
This edition published 2008
Text © 2000 Sheridan Cain
Illustrations © 2000 Jack Tickle
Sheridan Cain and Jack Tickle have asserted
their rights to be identified as the author
and illustrator of this work under the
Copyright, Designs and Patents Act, 1988.
Printed in China
All rights reserved
ISBN 978 1 84506 933 9
1 3 5 7 9 10 8 6 4 2

The Crunching Munching Caterpillar

Sheridan Cain
Jack Tickle

Caterpillar was always hungry. For weeks he crunched and munched his way through the fresh, juicy leaves of a blackberry bush.

One day, Caterpillar was about to crunch into another leaf when . . .

Bzzzzzzzzzzzz

Bumblebee landed
beside him!

"Wow!" said Caterpillar.
"How did you get here?"
"Simple," said Bumblebee.
"I have wings. Look!"
"Oh, I'd like some of those,"
said Caterpillar.

Bumblebee flew up into the air and buzzed busily from flower to flower.

Bzzzzz

Bzzzz

"I'd love to fly like that," said Caterpillar.
"Well, you can't," said Bumblebee.
"I've got wings, and you've got legs. Your legs are for walking."
"I guess so," sighed Caterpillar.

Bzzzzzoommm

Bumblebee flew off to the next bush.
Watching Bumblebee fly had made
Caterpillar *very* hungry, so he
crunched and he munched
until it was time for bed.

Crunch Munch
crunch Munch
yaw-w-n!

Caterpillar woke to
the sound of twittering.
Birds swooped and soared
in the early morning light.

Caterpillar was just about to start his breakfast when . . .

Sparrow landed
beside him.

"I'd love to fly high in the air like that," said Caterpillar.
"Well, you can't," said Sparrow. "You need to be as light as the dandelion fluff that floats on the breeze. You're far too big to fly. Your legs are for walking."
"I guess so," said Caterpillar sadly.

Caterpillar kept on crunching and munching
all day and into the evening, when the sun
began to set.

He wrapped a leaf around himself to keep warm.
He was just about to go to sleep when . . .

Butterfly landed gracefully beside him.
"Oh, I wish I could fly like you," sighed Caterpillar.
"But I'm too big and I have legs instead of wings."
Butterfly smiled a secret, knowing smile. "Who
knows? Perhaps one day you will fly,
light as a feather, like me," she said.
"But now, little Caterpillar, you should
go to sleep. You look very tired."

Butterfly was right. Caterpillar
suddenly felt very sleepy.
As Butterfly flew off into the
night sky, he fell into a deep,
deep sleep.

Caterpillar slept all through the winter,
and his sleep was filled with dreams.

He dreamed he had wings and was soaring in the blue sky above the tall trees . . . .

He dreamed he was a dandelion fluff, drifting toward the sun.

He dreamed he was as light as a feather, floating on the breeze.

When Caterpillar woke up he felt the warmth of the spring sun. He was stiff from his long sleep, but he did not feel very hungry. He **stretched** and **stretched**...

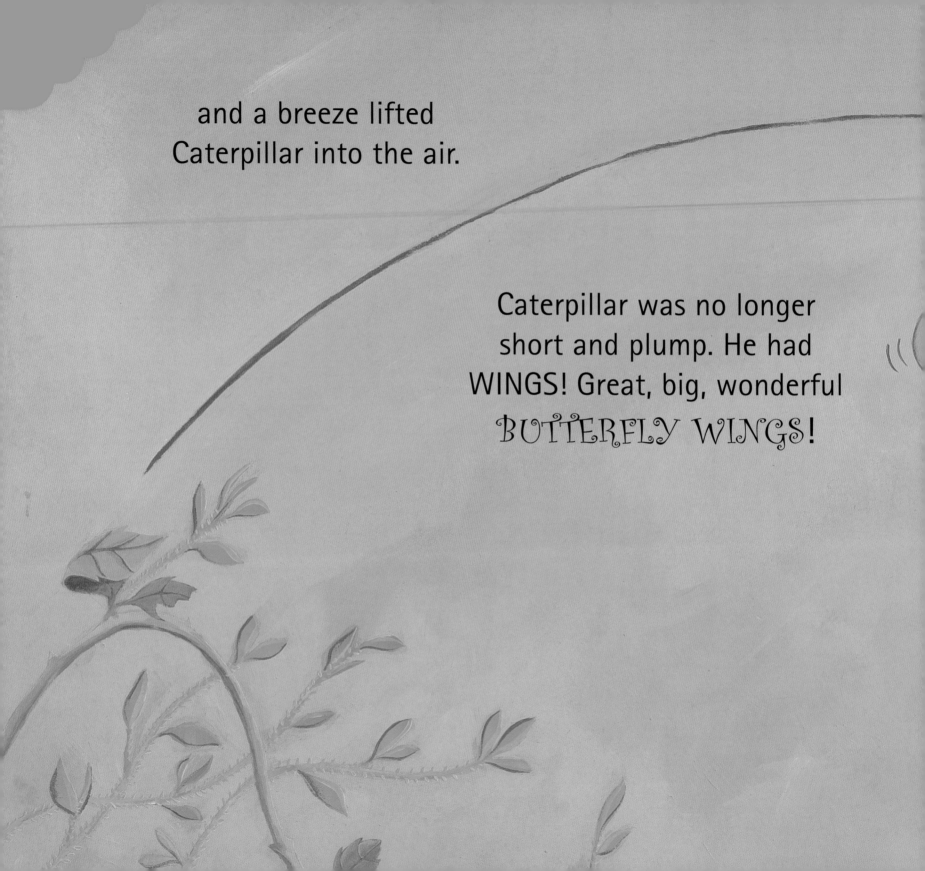

and a breeze lifted
Caterpillar into the air.

Caterpillar was no longer
short and plump. He had
WINGS! Great, big, wonderful
BUTTERFLY WINGS!

"Wow!" he said. "I'm flying! I'm really flying!"